Ar gyfer Jude. Gyda fy
nymuniadau gorau, diolch - J L

LITTLE TIGER PRESS LTD,
an imprint of the Little Tiger Group
I Coda Studios,
189 Munster Road,
London SW6 6AW
www.littletiger.co.uk

First published in France 2018
This edition published in Great Britain 2019

All rights reserved · ISBN 978-1-78881-098-2
Printed in China · LTP/1400/2402/0818

2 4 6 8 10 9 7 5 3 1

THE BIG ANGRY ROAR

Jonny Lambert

LITTLE TIGER

LONDON

As the pride patrolled,
the lion cubs squabbled.

First a push,

then a tumble,

followed by an "OW!"

"Stop it, you two! Cub, don't hurt your sister. You're old enough to know better!"

"But she started it!" snapped Cub.

And off he stomped.

"I'm so angry," scowled Cub. "I think I might **pop!**"

"Popping won't help!" giggled Gnu. "And it's terribly messy!" Zebra sniggered. "Listen, Cub, you have to learn to let your anger out."

"When we're angry, we **tramp** and **stamp**

and **STOMP!**"

Cub stamp-stomped up and down.

"Ouch! That hurt!" he angrily yelped.
"I stood on a stone. Stomping is stupid!"

Nursing a sore paw, Cub stormed off.
"I'm really angry now!" he shouted.
And he huffed and puffed and grumped!

"Oh, do stop with the boohoo!" snorted Rhino.
"You should do what we do," said Hippo.
"When we're annoyed . . ."

"... we

bash

and

crash,

Splatter and Splash!"

Cub charged up and down.

"Yuk! Now I'm smelly!" he bawled.

"Squelching and squishing is silly!"

Sulking and stinky, Cub clomped on . . .

SMACK!

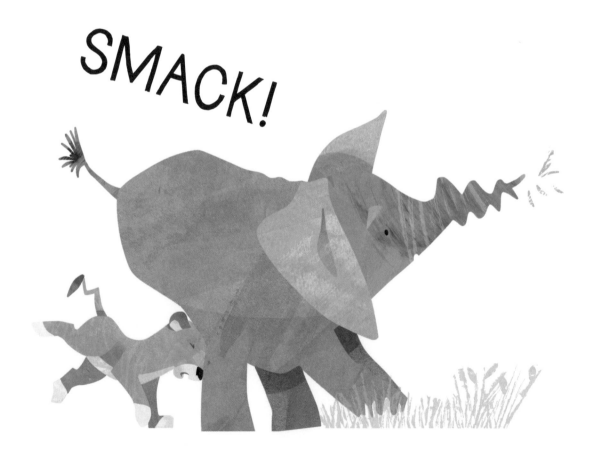

. . . straight into Elephant's bottom.

"Hey, you're in my way!" shouted Cub.

"TOOT!" trumpeted Elephant crossly.

"ROAR!" growled Cub angrily.

TOOT! TOOT!

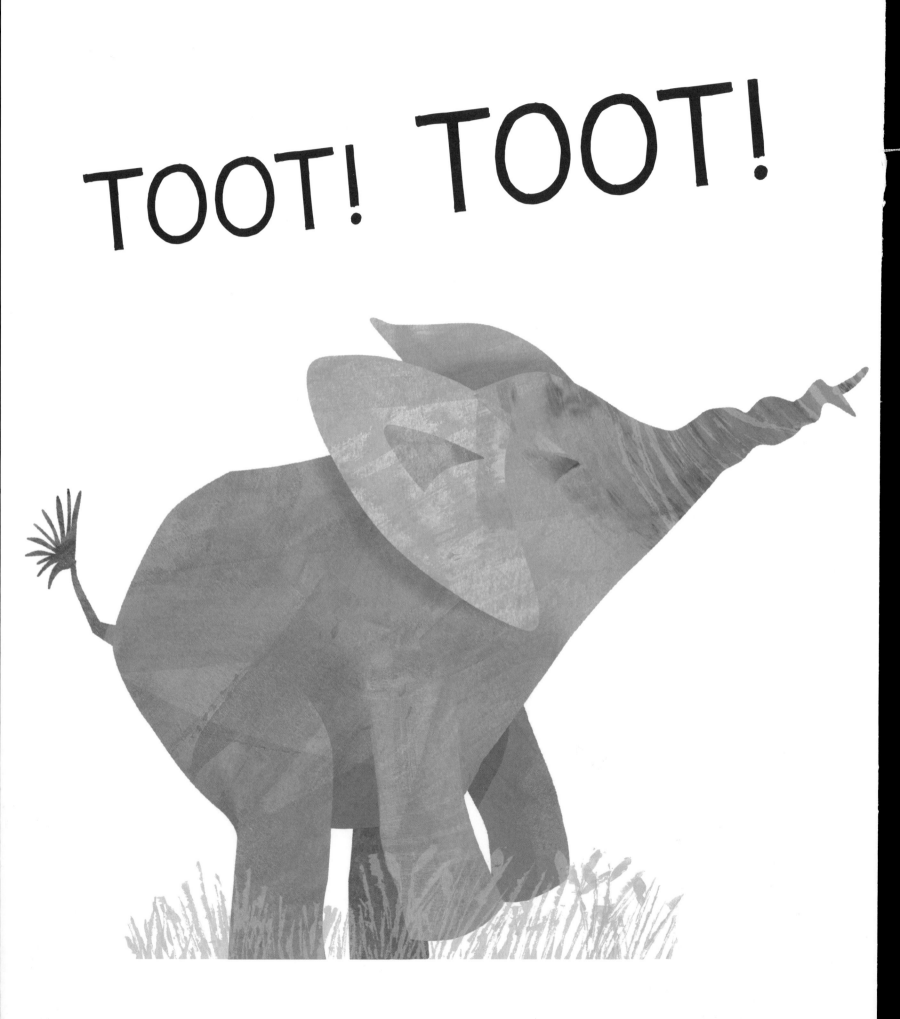

ROAR!

ROAR!

And they started
a massive . . .

STA

MPEDE!

"Oh no!" squeaked Cub.
"Did . . . did we do that?"
Baboon nodded.
He'd seen it all before.

"Everyone gets angry," smiled Baboon. "I do too. But I know how to let the anger out. Would you like to have a go?

First, breathe deeply in and out, and slowly count to ten."

"Pull lots of funny faces,

then start all over again!"

"I feel so much better," chuckled Cub.
"And my anger's gone. But I do
have something special to say . . ."

"Sorry."